BOUND TO THE DOCTOR

ASPEN RIDGE PACK: SHIFTER M.D.

LUNA WILDER

www.lunawilderbooks.com

WANT A FREE BOOK?

Want a free copy of Wolf Lover? It's a steamy, scarred military hero, curvy girl romance! Check it out today here!

*

He saved her life. She could be a little more grateful about it.

When Parker Bailey is brought into his emergency room, Jax Carson knows that he's just found his fated mate.

Unfortunately for him, her injuries are extensive, and he knows that modern medicine won't be enough to save her so he does the logical thing and bites her.

If only she saw it that way.

As soon as she's well enough to walk, she tries to leave him.

Jax has finally found his mate and he's not letting her go without a fight.

They're bound together. He only hopes that he can convince her that they're meant to be.

ONE

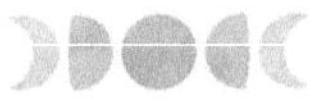

Jax

MICAH SIGHS as he leans on the front desk counter next to me. It's a slow night here at the Aspen Ridge Hospital. I just started my shift and I can already tell that it's going to be a boring night. I'm not looking forward to Micah sighing all night, and I wish I was working tonight with Roman instead. Though he would probably spend the whole shift talking about his mate, Iggy.

My wolf groans inside of me, pacing with barely restrained fury. He's been pissed with me a lot lately, and I know it's because we haven't gone out looking for our mate in a while. We used to go out one weekend a month when we were in college and medical school. We continued that tradition once we got back to Aspen Ridge, but then things got busy.

They're not busy right now, my wolf snarls, and I roll my eyes.

It's still winter here in Alaska, and it's hit or miss on if there will be a lot of people coming into the emergency room or not. There's still a bunch of tourists around, and I know that the ski lodge is booked for the next few weeks anyway. Shifters don't really get sick or have that many life-threatening emergencies because our animals give us fast healing properties, but it can still happen. Most people who come in are tourists who get hurt on the slopes or catch a cold.

"Are you just starting your shift?" My best friend, Roman, asks as he joins us at the front desk.

I met Roman when I first moved to Aspen Ridge and joined the pack here. He was the first friend that I made in town and in the hospital, and we became closer spending all of our long shifts bored together.

"Yeah, you're leaving soon, right?" I ask him.

"Yeah."

"How has it been?"

"Slow. I just finished my rounds. I have two patients in total," he says, and he sounds just as bored as I feel.

"How did you manage to handle the rush?" I joke, and he laughs.

I think that the reason why Roman and I get along so well is because we have the same type of personality. We're both matter-of-fact and serious. Our humor is dry, and our focus ever since we turned eighteen was to find our fated mate and graduate from medical school.

I've never had that before–someone who got me. I was a bit of a loner when I was younger. My parents were both lawyers and they spent most of their time working. That meant that I was on my own for most of my childhood.

Both of my parents were so methodical and oftentimes cold. They taught me to deal with the facts, and I grew up to be very analytical and abrupt, with no social skills. I couldn't relate to many kids my age.

I couldn't relate to my parents either. When I told them that I wanted to go to medical school instead of law school, they blew up. They wanted me to follow in their footsteps, and when I refused, they cut me off. I haven't spoken to them in years. I can't say that I really miss them.

I do miss having a family, though, of feeling like I belong somewhere and with someone. Aspen Ridge is my home now, but something is still missing.

Our mate, my wolf growls, and I swallow hard.

Roman's phone dings and he pulls it out of his white coat, smiling when he sees the message. I know without asking that it's his mate and new wife, Iggy. She came in last month after an avalanche hit the town, and Roman was luckily on duty. He bit her, saved her life, and they've been blissed out in love ever since.

What a lucky bastard.

My wolf growls inside of me, wanting us to make a plan to find our own mate, but I ignore him.

We'll find our mate soon. I'll take some time off and we can go looking for her. I promise.

He's not exactly thrilled with my compromise, but he stops growling at me so I'll take it.

A janitor walks by, yawning as he pushes his cart full of cleaning supplies to the storage closet, and Micah sighs again. His eyes cut to me, and I shake my head.

"No, I'm not covering for you again," I tell him before he can even ask.

When we're slow like this, I let Micah roam. Sometimes he runs home, especially if we're close to the end of our shift.

"We're not going to need both of us here tonight," he

tries to argue, and I shake my head.

"Then *I'll* leave," I suggest, and he glares at me.

"No, never mind," he grumbles, and I try to go back to ignoring him.

"If Asher were here, he would have done it," Micah grumbles, and I roll my eyes.

"Asher *is* here," I remind him.

"Oh yeah," he blinks. "Where did he disappear to?"

"I thought I saw him in the cafeteria," Roman says, barely looking up from his phone. "He was helping out in Pediatrics tonight, right?"

"Oh, yeah. I wonder if they need help," Micah says as he pushes off the front desk and starts to wander down the hall.

I shake my head. Out of the four of us, Micah is the one who can't handle the downtime the most. He gets bored easily. I'm not upset that he's wandering off. I know that if anything happens, at least he'll still be in the hospital.

The weather is clear tonight so the chances of a storm hitting or us having another avalanche happening are slim to none.

"I think I'm going to head out," Roman says, clapping me on the shoulder.

"Rub it in," I grumble, and he grins.

"It won't be that bad. Worst case, you can just take a nap," he says, and I nod.

"Tell Iggy that I said hi," I tell him, and he grins.

"Will do. See you later. Are you off tomorrow?" He asks as he starts to walk backwards down the hall.

"Yeah. I'll see you the day after."

He nods, raising his hand in a wave one last time before he hurries to the lockers to grab his stuff.

I cross my arms, looking around the quiet emergency

room. I have one patient who is still waiting for discharge papers but that's all. I've already checked on them, and they just need to sign the discharge papers that the nurse is about to bring them. The only other people here are Roman's two patients, and I know that he just looked in on them so there's not much for me to do.

Maybe I should take that nap...

I'm all caught up on my charts; I've answered all of my emails and the one voicemail that I had. Now there's nothing to do but wait for an emergency and stew about the fact that I don't have my own mate to go home to.

I'm glad for Roman. Truly, I am. He's a good guy, and I was actually there when he found her. I know they didn't have the easiest journey to their happily ever after, but they still figured it out. I'm happy for them. I just wish that I had found my mate by now too.

Maybe I should change departments. At least that way, I might not have so much downtime. I could only work days and have a set schedule.

The doors bang open at the end of the hall, and my wolf and I go on high alert instantly. We've got a patient! I shouldn't be so happy about that, but at least it will give me something to do. I stop the nurse before she can greet them.

"I'll get it," I tell her.

It doesn't even matter what it is. I will take care of it. I need something to pull me away from my thoughts before the jealousy threatens to drown me.

My wolf snarls in my head, and I ignore him, pushing away from the desk and heading to where the EMT is wheeling in someone on a stretcher.

"Skiing accident, she hit her femoral artery. She's lost a lot of blood," he tells me, and I nod, grabbing gloves and pulling them on as I take over for the other EMT.

I'm listening to him rattle off shorthand for everything they did on the ride to the hospital. Nurses are running around, and I start to get lost in the blur of caring for a new patient when I stop dead in my tracks.

What is that? What's that scent? It's like sugar and—

MATE! My wolf howls in my head, and my teeth start to elongate.

Now? I can't believe that this is happening now. Fate sure does have a funny sense of humor.

I can't seem to stop breathing in her sugary sweet scent. It's like a drug hitting my system, and my mind is blank from everything except biting her.

I blink, shaking my head and trying to focus on the task at hand.

"We need to stop the bleeding," I say as the EMTs head back out to their ambulance. "We need a surgical suite!" I yell out as we start to move.

The nurses are bustling around me, and I focus on my mate. Her black hair is mussed from her knit hat, and she looks so pale. I need to stop the bleeding, but when I pull back the sheet to get a good look at the cut, I know that's going to be hard.

The EMTs must have cut off her snow pants and jeans because she's just in her underwear. My wolf is begging me to bite her. It would save her life and we would be able to claim her, but I hold him off.

There could be humans around; I remind him. *We have to do this the medical way first.*

We get her wheeled into a surgical suite and I scrub in as fast as possible before I begin the procedure. I have to create a graft to replace where the artery was cut, and we need to get her blood pressure back up. I'm sure that she's going to need more than a few transfusions too.

"Check her blood type and hang a bag!" I order as I get started on the graft.

My eyes keep straying to her face as I work, and I try my best to focus. The beeping of the monitors echo around the room, and I swallow hard.

I can't lose her. I just found her.

My wolf is back pacing inside me, and I can feel how anxious he is. It's only amplifying my own anxiety, and I swallow hard. I shake my head, going back to focusing on the surgery. I get the graft in place just as the monitors start to go crazy.

"Blood pressure is dropping fast," one of the nurses calls, and I reach for the paddles as she calls off the quickly dropping numbers.

"We're going to need more blood in here!" I yell, and they race to get more bags.

I look around the room, taking in the nurses present and making sure that there's no one else watching. I know that I could shock her and maybe get her heart rate to return, but if that doesn't work, then it's going to be too late. If I'm going to bite her, now is the time to do it.

All of the nurses in the room are shifters, and when they see my elongated teeth, they all step back.

"Is she..." one of them asks, and I nod.

"She's mine, my fated mate. I'm not going to lose her. Make sure that no one is watching," I whisper to her, and she hurries to make sure that the door is closed tightly and there's no one nearby.

My wolf licks his lips in excitement, but I can still sense his fear as I lean over our mate and take another deep breath. Her scent hits me, mixed in with her blood, and I close my eyes as I sink my teeth into her smooth flesh.

I can only hope that it's enough to bring her back to me.

TWO

Parker

THEY MUST HAVE *me on some good pain medicine because I had some crazy dreams. I don't even feel any pain.*

That's my first thought when I wake up in the hospital the next morning. It has to be really early because the room is almost pitch black, with no sunlight peeking in from behind the blinds.

I blink my eyes open, letting my eyes adjust to the darkness as I try to piece together what happened and where I am.

The where I am part is easy. The beeping of the machines next to me kind of gives it away. I spent a lot of time in hospitals when my mom was sick, and I would recognize the sound of the heart monitor machine anywhere.

The what happened part is less clear. Pieces of the accident and ambulance ride are clear in my head, but the rest is a jumbled mess. I remember gaining consciousness a few times, but never for very long.

A dark-haired man keeps popping up. He's got piercing blue eyes, and he's staring at me so intently that his look is almost like a brand on my skin. I could almost swear he bit me, but that can't be right. There's no memory of him leaning down or of much of anything. It's just of him licking his lips after he had sunk his teeth into me.

Doctors don't do that, though, and the man in my dreams was wearing a white coat and scrubs like one so I know it couldn't have happened.

I shift in the bed and try not to cry out. My body feels sore like I was hit by a truck, but only when I move. I can clearly remember hitting that tree, though. There was so much blood in the snow around me, the red spreading across the while snow surprisingly fast. I'm just lucky that a couple was skiing downhill behind me and came to check on me; otherwise I'm sure I would have died on that mountain before anyone stumbled upon me.

I should find them and thank them.

I squint my eyes, trying to make out anything in the dark room. There's a figure to my left, dozing softly in the chair there. For one second, I think that it's my dad, but the shape is too lean and narrow.

Where are my dad and Susan? Shouldn't they be here? Would the hospital really kick them out? Maybe they didn't know to call them and let them know that I was brought in?

I doubt that's what happened here. It's actually more likely that they didn't even bother coming to the hospital to check on me.

My dad just married Susan a few weeks ago. It was a spur-of-the-moment decision for me. I hadn't even met her yet when he told me that he was engaged and then married.

I had been away at culinary school for a few months, and then, bam! I came home to a new stepmother.

My dad is crazy about her, but I can't say the same. I don't get what he sees in her. She's selfish and abrasive. She also seems like she hates me. If my dad shows me any attention, she glares at me and does everything in her power to get him to focus on her instead.

He actually missed my graduation last week because she had an emergency. Well, what they said was an emergency. They still won't tell me what exactly happened. This little ski trip was supposed to be his way to make it up to me and for Susan and me to bond.

So far, it's been a disaster.

I sigh, trying not to think about my evil stepmother. I mean, I graduated. I could get a job in a kitchen or bakery somewhere. I could move far away and never have to deal with her again.

The idea of never seeing Susan again actually sounds amazing, but I hate to think that if that happened, I would also have to avoid seeing my dad. It had always been just the two of us growing up. My mom died from breast cancer when I was just ten, and my dad was the only parent I ever had. We were always so close. That's what makes losing him to her so hard.

I mean, I want him to be happy, and he seems to be with Susan. I just wish that I didn't hate his new wife so much.

I thought maybe I just disliked her because she was taking him away from me, so I really tried to give her a chance. That's not it, though. Susan is a gossip who loves stirring up trouble. She's self-centered and manipulative. We just have nothing in common.

I was actually trying to get a break from them and went down the wrong hill. That's what led to all of this.

At least now I'll have an excuse to dip out of all the activities they had planned for us. I can enjoy my swanky room at the ski lodge and order room service.

My fingers brush against my leg, and I can feel a small bandage there. It seems weird. There was so much blood, and I could have sworn that the gash was bigger. Shouldn't the wound be bigger? I wish I could turn on the lights and look at it.

A nurse comes in, and I get a brief look at the room when the door opens.

"Hey there," she says, and I smile.

"Hi."

"I'm just here to give you some more medicine," she says.

"The good stuff?" I joke, and she smiles as she injects something into the IV bag hanging next to me.

"Of course," she says, winking, and I laugh.

I want to ask her where my dad is or to turn on a light, but the pain medicine really must be the strong stuff because it's starting to make me sleepy already. She heads back to the door, and I turn to the figure in the chair, trying to make out who it could be.

She opens the door, and the light from the hallway spills in. My eyes lock with a pair of piercing blue ones, and I gasp.

It's him. The doctor from my dreams. The man who bit me.

He's real?

My hand goes to where he bit me in my dreams, and I half moan, half gasp again when I feel the ridge of a bite mark there.

"It wasn't a dream," I mumble, my eyelids starting to droop even more.

"Sleep, mate. You need your rest now. We'll talk soon," he promises.

His voice washes over me like a soothing wave, and I try to fight it, but it's no use. My eyelids slip closed, and my thoughts turn once more to a handsome doctor promising me that everything is going to be okay.

"You're mine now, mate. I've got you," he whispers, and I try to figure out if that was real or a dream as I fall deeper asleep.

THREE

Jax

I'VE BEEN WATCHING my mate sleep for hours. I wish that she was awake by now. I wish I had thought to ask her for her name when she was awake in the middle of the night, but I wasn't thinking clearly. My wolf and I are fine with just calling her mate, but I think humans and people with better social skills like to be referred to by their names.

My shift is almost over now, and I know that I need to go check on the few other patients. I was able to text Micah and get him to cover for me. I still need to do rounds before I leave for the day.

I've been hesitating to leave my mate's side because I want to be here when she wakes up to answer any questions she has. The pain medicine should be wearing off soon, and I know she'll be awake then.

As if on cue, her eyelids start to flutter and she blinks her blue eyes open, looking around the room until her eyes land on me. My wolf sits up inside me, his tail twitching happily as we stare at our mate.

"Morning," I say gruffly.

"Hi," she says, and she looks uncertain about what to say next.

I wish that I was better at this. I wish I was charming or had the skills to put her at ease and make her like me instantly.

"I'm your mate... and your doctor," I finish lamely. "Do you remember last night?" I ask her.

"Um, kind of. It's all just like a kaleidoscope in my head.," she says, and I nod.

"I'm not surprised. You lost a lot of blood."

"I'm surprised that I made it."

"Well, you almost didn't. I had to bite you when your heart stopped."

Her eyes bulge out, and I realize that maybe I shouldn't have said that. I should have softened that bit of information or just kept it to myself.

"You'll be fine now," I rush to add.

I can't believe it, but it's just now dawning on me that she's not a shifter. I was so wrapped up in saving her and then just so happy that my wolf and I had finally found our mate that I didn't even think about the fact that another shifter wouldn't have needed my bite to help heal.

This isn't good. I was counting on my mate being a shifter and falling in love with me the moment that she smelled me. What do I do now? I don't stand a chance with this girl. She's beautiful.

She probably already has a boyfriend.

My wolf snarls in my head, and I find myself baring my teeth at the idea of another man touching my woman.

Well, that's okay. I'll need to rework the next few hours

to explain shifters and fated mates, but that's okay. I'm already planning the speech and everything that she'll need to know about wolf shifters and the pack.

It's all going to work out. Nothing can get me down now that we have our fated mate.

"We should talk," I start, scooting my chair closer to her bedside.

"Oh god. Am I dying?" She asks, her eyes wide with fear.

"No!"

Okay, maybe things aren't going to be okay... How am I messing this up so badly?

"No, you're going to be fine. You'll have to take it easy for a day or two, but you're going to survive. My bite saved you."

"So, you did bite me," she says in an accusatory tone.

Her hand goes to the bite mark at the base of her neck, and she looks at me like I'm a psycho.

"I'm a wolf shifter. Have you heard of shifters?"

"Uh, no..."

"It's a person that can change into an animal," I tell her.

She's still staring at me like I'm crazy, and I wonder if I'm being too blunt. I've been told that sometimes I don't have the best bedside manner.

"I'm a wolf. There's actually a lot of wolf shifters in this town."

"Uh-huh," she says, her eyes darting to the door like she's praying for someone to walk in and save her from this conversation.

"I'm Jax," I say, trying to get the conversation back to a good place. "What's your name? We didn't have that much information when you came in."

"I'm Parker. Wait, was my dad not here with me?"

"Um, no. The EMTs brought you in by yourself."

She looks away from me, and I can see the tears forming in her eyes.

"Maybe he doesn't know yet? What's his name and number? I'll find him and let him know that you're here."

"No, it's fine. When can I leave?"

"You should be discharged soon. Maybe later today or tomorrow."

My wolf is tense inside me. We both hate the thought of her leaving us.

She just meant when can she be discharged; I try to reassure us both.

"Um, back to the shifter thing," I say, clearing my throat. "There's one more thing that we need to talk about."

"What?" She asks, clearly still distracted.

"We're mates. We're literally fated to be together. That's why I bit you. I had to claim you, but it also gave you some of my shifter properties, like the ability to heal faster."

"Uh-huh," she says, and I relax in my seat.

This is going better than I thought it would.

I smile as the door opens, and Roman sticks his head in.

"Hey, got a second?" He asks, and I nod.

"I'll be back in a minute," I tell Parker, and she stares at me a little blankly as I head for the door.

"I heard that you found your mate," Roman says with a grin, and I nod.

"Yeah, she was brought in right after you left for the night."

"And?" He asks.

"And she's human. I bit her last night, and we just talked about shifters and fated mates."

"Yeah? How did that go?" He asks.

"Really good."

"Really," he says in disbelief, and I nod.

"Yeah."

"Are you sure?"

"She seems on board with all of this."

"Did she ask any questions? What did she say?"

"She said 'okay.'"

"Oh, Jax," Roman says, and I frown.

"What?"

"That conversation did not go well. She probably thinks that you're crazy. I told Iggy about shifters and fated mates and had Rue tell her about them too, and I still had to shift in front of her for Iggy to believe that I was a wolf shifter. Then it took even longer to prove that we were meant to be. There's no way your mate is already on board with all of that."

I know Roman bit his mate without asking and was so nervous about her being mad about that, but it all worked out for him. I'm sure that it will be the same for me too.

"You're wrong. You'll see. She's in love with me already," I tell him, but as I turn back to my mate, I can't help but wonder if Roman is right.

Am I messing this all up?

FOUR

Parker

OKAY, *so he's insane.*

I wonder if I'm on the psychiatric floor for some reason...

I try to push thoughts of the strange man from my head as I take stock of my injuries. I'm hesitant to peel back the bandage and see the wound. Blood and gore have always freaked me out, but I force myself to.

Something just feels off. I mean, I lost a lot of blood on that mountain. I ran into a tree. Shouldn't I be sore and weak? Yet I feel like I could walk out of here right now just fine.

I take a deep breath, close my eyes and try to keep myself from getting dizzy or freaking out as I slowly peel the edge of the bandage back.

"What the hell?" I ask.

The door to my hospital room opens, and I expect it to be Dr. Crazy back for more nonsense, but instead, my dad and Susan come strolling in.

My dad shoots me an apologetic look, but I'm too confused by everything that has happened this morning to pay him much mind right now. My teeth are already gritting at the sight of Susan, and I take a deep breath, preparing to deal with her.

I don't get what my dad sees in her. With my mom they were always laughing together and smiling. My mom was hilarious, and I always wanted a love like theirs. So, how did my dad go from that kind of love with my mom to Susan?

"See? I told you that she was just being dramatic," Susan says as she looks down at my leg.

There's barely a scratch there, and I frown harder.

"This isn't right," I murmur. "I remember the size of the cut last night. This is nothing. This isn't right."

"Uh huh," Susan says, taking a noisy sip of her coffee.

"What happened, honey?" My dad asks, and I try not to roll my eyes.

I want to yell at him. I want to demand where he was and why he's just now showing up, but I'm too drained for the fight that I know would ensue. I just want to get out of here and go back to the ski lodge. I need to think things through quietly.

"She's so dramatic. Here we are, trying to give her a good trip, trying to bond with her, and she's faking an injury to get all the attention back on herself. I told you, Doug. I told you that was what happened," Susan drones on, and I place the bandage back on my leg, gritting my teeth to stop from saying the retort that is on the tip of my tongue.

A nurse comes back in, giving me a friendly smile, and I clear my throat.

"Can I be discharged now?" I ask her.

"Let's just check out a few things," she says, removing a corner of the bandage to check out the scar.

Her eyes flash, and I shake my head, watching to see if they'll do it again or if it was just a trick of the light.

"Looking a lot better. You gave us quite the scare last night," she says.

"So, it was bad?" My dad asks, and she nods.

"Oh, yes. We had to give her quite a few transfusions. She should be good to go home now. You'll need to take it easy the next few days. No more skiing for you, I'm afraid. I'll get the doctor to sign off on your discharge paperwork."

With that, she heads out of the room, and I kick off the covers. My clothes are nowhere to be seen, and I briefly remember them being cut off me. There's a set of folded scrubs on a nearby chair, and I grab them, heading into the bathroom to change.

I stare at my reflection in the mirror above the tiny sink, taking in the dark circles under my eyes and how pale I look. I'm sure that the paleness is from the loss of blood. I look surprisingly well for someone who almost died a few hours ago.

My eyes stray to the slightly raised red bite mark at the base of my neck. I had seen it when I first took off the hospital gown, but I tried to convince myself that I was imagining it, that it was a mirage. It's real though.

My fingers smooth over the mark, and a shiver runs down my neck.

Maybe that crazy man was telling the truth?

Nope, I shake my head. I can't even begin to think about what he said. Not right now, anyway. I need to get out of here, get away from my dad and Susan. Then I'll deal with it.

My black hair is mussed from the thin hospital pillow, and I run my fingers through it, trying to comb it out. My blue eyes look bright and maybe a little wild. I know that I slept a lot last night, but I'm still exhausted.

Let's get the heck out of here.

I leave the hospital gown hanging on the hook on the back of the bathroom door and head out to deal with this mess.

"Here's those discharge papers," the nurse says, and I hurry to sign them. "You need to take it easy for the next few days."

I nod at the reminder and finish signing the last page.

"I'm all set to go?" I ask, and she nods.

"Yes, here's your aftercare notes," she says, and I shove the papers into my pocket. "And here's your belongings."

She holds up a plastic bag with my cell phone and room key in it.

"Thanks," I tell her honestly, and she gives me a smile.

"Take care of yourself, honey," she says, and I nod again.

"Can we go now?" Susan whines, and my dad wraps his arm around her waist.

"I'm sure that Parker is excited to get back to the ski lodge and rest for a bit," he says.

"Good. Then we can hit the slopes again," Susan coos up at him.

Their concern for me is touching, really.

I follow behind them as we make our way toward the front door. Every time I see someone in a white coat, I find myself ducking my head and trying to avoid them.

I'm feeling overwhelmed with everything that's happened in the last twelve hours, and I know that I can't handle anything else that he's going to say to me right now.

I need to rest. Scratch that; I need a shower and then to

rest. Then I'll analyze what he said and why I had such a strong reaction to him.

I follow my dad and Susan out into the early morning sunlight and try to put the last twelve hours out of my head.

At least for a little bit.

FIVE

Jax

I THOUGHT I would be back to my mate in a few minutes. Instead, it's an hour later and the end of my shift by the time I make it back to her room.

My wolf has been going crazy inside of me ever since we left her, and I can't blame him. We've finally found our mate, and we don't want to be away from her for a second.

I got pulled out because Roman wanted to ask me about Parker, and then we had a family come in. They were all sick with food poisoning, but we had to run a few tests. Now I'm clocked out and beelining it back to my mate.

I need to check on her, but I also want to see if I'm right about us being on the same page. What Roman said earlier has been stuck in my head. I need to see if maybe I read the room wrong with Parker earlier.

I hope that I was right. I don't know another way to explain that we're meant to be to Parker or how to make her see that.

"Sorry, that took so..." I trail off as I look around the empty room.

It's already been cleaned, and I know then that Parker must have left a while ago. My wolf snarls at me, and I grit my teeth.

We'll get her back; I promise him as he starts to prowl inside of me.

Why would she just leave? I guess our little talk this morning really didn't go as well as I thought it did...

Obviously, I won't be sharing that piece of information with Roman. I'd never hear the end of it.

I step out into the hallway, looking around for any sign of her.

"When did she discharged?" I snap at the first nurse that passes by me.

"Um, I'm not sure," she stammers, and I stalk off to the front desk when I remember that she was skiing.

She's at the ski lodge.

I spin on my heel, hurrying to the lockers to grab my things, and then I jog outside to my car. A light dusting of snow is covering it, and a few more flurries are still coming down.

My wolf and I are both starting to get worried. What if she got hurt trying to drive around town? She shouldn't have left. She should have waited for us. We're meant to take care of her now. Doesn't she get that? Obviously not or she wouldn't have left.

We'll just have to explain it to her.

The drive to the ski lodge goes by in the blink of an eye. I'm too busy trying to figure out what I'm going to say to her when I see her to pay attention to the road. Luckily for me, there's never really any traffic in Aspen Ridge.

I park out front of the hotel side of the ski lodge and jog

inside. Kale is behind the front desk, looking bored. He's one of the younger pups in our pack, and he's always looked up to me for some reason so I know he'll give me my mate's room number without a fight.

"Kale," I say, and he snaps his head up.

"Jax! Hey, man. What are you doing here? Need a room?"

"I need a room number, actually. Her name is Parker, but I don't have a last name."

Should have checked her discharge papers before I came here.

"Sure, man. Give me just a second."

I lean on the counter, impatiently waiting for him to give me the information. He's busy typing away on the computer, and he frowns.

"There isn't a guest named Parker here," he tells me, and I growl.

"She has to be here. She was brought in last night after a ski accident. She was just released this morning," I snap at him.

"Oh! Black hair? Curvy?" He asks, and I growl again.

My wolf and I don't like other men commenting on our mate or her curves.

"Yes," I say harshly. "Where is she?"

"She came in with her parents. Hold on; I think I have their room number here."

He starts typing again, and I hold my wolf back from jumping over this counter and doing it myself. I know that he can find it faster.

"Rooms 312 and 314," he tells me, holding up a room key. "The couple was in 312, so here is the key to 314."

"Thanks, Kale. I owe you one," I tell him as I grab the key and head for the elevator.

There's a small line there, and I can feel my wolf is close to breaking free. I push into the stairwell, using all my anger and anxiety at losing my mate to push me up the three flights of stairs and onto the third floor.

I knock on the door, waiting impatiently for her to answer it. I'm two seconds from breaking the door down when I remember the key card. It flashes green, and I rush into the room. It isn't until I'm in her room that I realize she might not appreciate me breaking into her room like this.

Am I going to be driving her further away?

It's too late to stop now.

The bed is empty, and for a minute, I wonder if Kale gave me the wrong room number. Her scent is all over this place, though. My wolf and I inhale deeply, loving her sweet bubble gum and sugar scent.

The water turns on in the shower, and I'm instantly in motion. I push open the bathroom door and finally relax when my eyes lock on my curvy mate.

"Parker," I say, and she turns with a shriek.

"What are you doing? Get out!" She yells, and I prowl closer.

I can't really make out her from the neck down because of the opaque glass, but the hint of her beautiful body is there, causing my wolf and I to go hard all over.

"I told you to wait for me," I say, trying to hide my raging hard-on.

I need to think with a clear head so that I don't mess this up with her.

"And I told you to get out!"

"We're mates. You can't just be running around without me. Plus, you're supposed to be resting," I tell her.

"I'm serious. Get. Out."

"We need to talk. We need to go over a few things," I say, crossing my arms over my chest.

I'm not moving from this spot until we've gone over some ground rules. She must still have questions. I can answer them, and then we'll get back on track.

"You should be resting, preferably under my watchful eye."

"I just wanted to take a shower in peace," she groans.

"Come out. You need to rest. We can talk in bed."

"Get out. I'll talk to you after I get dressed," she counters.

I mull over her offer, my eyes straying to her silhouette. My mouth waters at the sight, and my wolf licks his lips.

There's no doubt that we want her. Convincing her that she belongs to us might be harder than we first thought, so it would help to get on her good side.

"Fine. You have two minutes," I tell her, holding up two fingers.

"Uh-huh, now get out!"

I head back out to the hotel room, sitting down on the bed, my back straight as I practice what I want to say to her in my head.

Her things are still neatly folded in the open suitcase on the dresser, and I smile. Good, that will make moving her into my place easier.

The shower turns off a minute later, and I sit up straighter. It's game time, and this is one game that I don't plan on losing.

SIX

Parker

I CAN'T BELIEVE *that he broke into my hotel room. How did he even find me?*

Those are the types of questions running through my mind as I hurry to tug on my pajamas and go out to face him.

I know that I should probably be afraid. I mean, a strange man just broke into my hotel room, but surely if he wanted to kidnap me, he would have done it when I was in the shower. Instead, he left.

Well, not left, I think as I step out of the bathroom and see him on the bed. I realize it isn't fear buzzing along my skin but something else. Something like excitement.

"Why are you here?" I ask.

I had decided it would be best to take the lead with the questioning here. I have a feeling that it's not going to go well, though.

"You weren't supposed to leave the hospital. I told you.

We're mates. We're meant to be together. I thought that you got that."

"Listen, I think you might need psychological help."

He sighs, glowering at me as he stands and starts to pull off his shirt. Actually, maybe that isn't a glower. It might just be his normal face.

Resting grumpy doctor face.

I smile at my own joke and try to get back on track.

"Okay, now I know that you need psychological help."

"I'm going to show you. I'll shift for you, and then you'll believe me."

"And you need to take your shirt off for that. Oh! And your pants, apparently too," I say when he reaches for the button of his pants.

"I'll tear my clothes if I shift with them on," he explains matter-of-factly, and he makes it sound like it should be obvious.

"Right, right," I say, averting my eyes when he pushes his pants and boxers down his legs.

I stare at the ceiling, wondering how my life got to this point. I used to be an average, normal girl. I had my whole future in front of me. Now I'm standing in a hotel room a thousand miles from home with a naked man that bit me last night.

Maybe I should try to run. I could get out in the hallway and scream for help. It might work.

"Ready?"

"Sure?" I say, and it sounds more like a question than a response.

"Okay, it will be fast," he warns, and I nod.

Curiosity gets the better of me, and I look down, watching in astonishment as his hair starts to grow longer. It seems like it all happens in the blink of an eye. One second, he's human and standing naked in front of me; the next second, he's a huge wolf.

"Oh, shit..." I wheeze, stumbling back a step.

Okay, so the dude isn't crazy. I mean, this whole situation is bonkers, but he's at least not insane.

I feel like I don't know where to look. He's standing patiently, and I find myself taking a step closer to him. I reach my hand out, and he pushes his head into it.

I let out a breath that I didn't even realize I was holding. His fur is so soft and thick, and I run my fingers through it. The wolf nudges me again, and I laugh.

What am I doing?

"Alright, you're a wolf. Or a shifter. Whatever it's called," I say, forcing myself to take a step back.

He shifts back, and I'm too shocked by what just happened to look away this time.

"Now that you believe me, we should get your things. I can show you around our home."

"What?"

"We're mates. We're bound together now. We have to be together. You can rest and get settled into our place. You should be resting."

"I... I don't live here. I'm not moving in with you."

"We're *fated mates*," he stresses, and I stare at him blankly.

"We're *strangers*," I remind him.

He frowns, obviously not liking that answer.

"Come home with me," he tries again, his words sounding more like an order this time.

"No."

He growls, glaring at me, and I glare right back.

"Fine. Then I'm staying here with you."

"That's really not necessary."

"We're bound together. We have been ever since I bit you. I saved your life by marking you. You could be a little more grateful about that, by the way."

"Oh my God!" I shout, but he ignores me.

"We're meant to be."

"You keep saying that, but I don't believe it. How can you be so sure about that?"

"I'm a shifter. That's how this happens for us."

"Okay, well, I'm new to all of this. I need you to walk me through it so I can try to wrap my head around all of this."

"Okay, I will. Just sit down. You should be resting."

I have a feeling that he's about to pick me up and tuck me into bed himself, so I reluctantly crawl onto the bed. The truth is that I am still sore and tired. The hot shower helped ease some of the aches, but it's coming back now.

"I get that you were telling the truth about being a shifter and that this is how it works for you, but it's not how us humans do it. We date and develop feelings."

"We can go on dates, but it's fated to be. We're meant to be together. The feelings, the bond, it's already there."

"It's not for me," I tell him firmly.

I'm tired and grouchy. I'm starting to get sick of having to argue with him and repeat myself.

"They're not there *yet*."

I roll my eyes, and he takes a seat on the edge of the bed.

"I'm going to prove it to you. You didn't believe me about being a wolf shifter, but I proved it to you. This won't be any different. The mating moon is coming up soon. You'll feel it then."

"I'm leaving in three days and going back home," I tell him firmly.

"You won't. You'll be in love with me by then," he says smugly.

"Oh my gosh," I groan, collapsing back against the pillows.

"Three days. I promise," he says, and I stare up at the ceiling.

I guess there's no harm in giving him a chance. It sure beats hanging out with my dad and Susan.

"Fine. Three days," I say weakly, giving in to him.

"Challenge accepted," he says, and I can see in his eyes that he means it.

For some reason, that determined look in his eyes only turns me on, and I wonder just how crazy the next few days are going to be.

SEVEN

Jax

THE COUCH in Parker's hotel room is surprisingly comfortable, but my wolf and I would still rather be in bed with our mate. We spent half the night just listening to her breathing. It was comforting somehow, but I think if I were to tell her that, she wouldn't like it.

How am I going to do this? I was so confident last night when we were talking, but the truth is that it was all an act. I can't read a typical situation with low stakes. How am I going to navigate the next few days with Parker?

I can't lose my mate; I just can't.

Doubt and worry eat at me, and I sit up in bed. Pacing helps me think. Maybe it will help me figure out a plan to win over my mate.

I start my path at the foot of her bed, walking over to the hotel door and then back to the couch under the window.

I need to court her, woo her. Do people still call it that?

My shoulders droop. I'm going to lose her for sure.

Parker seems cool. She's never going to fall for an antisocial loser like me.

My wolf growls inside me, shaking his head, and I roll my shoulders back, resuming my pacing.

He's right. We have to try. We both know that living without her now that I've bitten her isn't an option.

We could try to just lay out all of the facts again.

God, my parents would be so thrilled to see me thinking like a lawyer, I think bitterly.

They probably wouldn't have been much help in this situation either. I could ask Roman, but I know he's wrapped up in his mate right now. Micah and Asher still haven't found their mates, so I doubt they would be much help in this situation.

I turn around and start walking back to the window, frustration starting to build inside of me. My wolf is pacing back and forth inside of me, and I can feel his own stress levels spiking.

It's not helping things.

Okay, focus. What about laying out all of the facts again? It didn't work last night, but maybe it will now that she's slept on things?

Somehow, I doubt it, but I still have to try. My wolf snorts inside of me, and I sigh again. He's right. This is doomed.

"Are you planning ways to kill me?" Parker asks from the bed, and I jump, turning to face her.

"What? No, of course not. You're my mate. I would never hurt you," I promise her as I move closer to the bed.

"What's with all of the pacing, then?" She asks through a yawn as she sits up.

"It helps me think."

"What were you thinking so hard about?"

She blinks her pretty blue eyes up at me, and my heart starts to race in my chest. This girl, she's mine. She's *fated* to be mine. She has to love me. Right? Maybe I don't need to try too hard or overthink things. Maybe I just need to trust my gut and fate.

"You," I croak out.

"Murdering me," she asks slowly, and I roll my eyes.

"No, I swear. I'll never hurt you."

"Okay, well, just so you know, sighing and pacing around the room of the girl you kind of tried to kidnap the night before is giving off major serial killer vibes."

"I'll work on that," I deadpan, and to my surprise, she laughs.

The sound is like a melody, and my wolf sits up straighter inside me.

Make her do it again! He growls at me, and I search my brain, trying to figure out how to make that happen.

I've never been great at making people laugh, but maybe I could try to learn how. I'd do anything if it meant making Parker fall in love with me.

"Parker? Are you up, sweetie?" A man asks, knocking on the hotel door.

My wolf and I both growl at the same time, and Parker rolls her eyes.

"Down, boy. It's just my dad."

"Oh," I say, relaxing.

She throws the blankets off, and I'm at her side at once.

"How are you feeling?" I ask, my eyes roaming over her.

"I'm fine. I promise."

I nod, hovering near her side as she stands and heads to the door.

"Yeah, I'm up, dad. Just getting dressed."

"Hurry up! We're starving," comes a female voice, and I bare my teeth again.

"I don't like the way she talks to you," I tell Parker, and she blinks, a pretty pink flush staining her cheeks.

"Me either," she admits quietly, and I move closer to her side.

She's digging through her suitcase, and I watch as she pulls out some black yoga pants and a thick wool sweater.

"I'll help you change," I say, and she laughs again.

"Nice try," she says, and even though she's rejecting me, I light up inside.

I made her laugh again! Maybe I can actually do this.

"Just a second!" She calls out to her dad and that woman.

She heads into the bathroom, and I tidy up the hotel room for her as she changes. The bathroom door opens, and I snarl when I see Parker.

"No."

"What?" She asks, looking confused.

"You can't wear that," I tell her, and she frowns down at her clothes.

"Why not?"

She turns around, trying to see the back of her pants, and I growl again, my cock hardening in my pants as we take in the way that the tight yoga pants mold to each and every one of her curves.

"Too much of you is showing," I tell her, and she looks at me like I'm crazy.

"I'm literally covered from my ankles to my neck."

"It's too... revealing. Everyone will be staring at you, at what's mine. They'll want you," I tell her, my eyes sliding down her body to those damn leggings.

She laughs again, rolling her eyes , and I glare at her.

"No one is going to be looking at me. Trust me."

"They will. You are the most beautiful woman in the world. They will all be staring at you and imagining doing dirty things to you," I half snarl.

"Is that what you're doing?" She asks softly, a speculative look in her eyes, and I swallow hard.

"Yes," I admit. "How could I not when you look like this."

My wolf and I are both practically drooling as she tugs on her socks and shoes. She bends over, flipping her suitcase closed, and I moan out loud.

"You're trying to make me suffer," I say miserably, and she smiles.

"I'm about to go eat with my dad and evil stepmom. It will be fine."

"I don't like her," I say, glaring at the door.

"I don't either, but my dad does so," she shrugs, and I shake my head.

"Then I don't like him either. He should be protecting you. Especially from his own wife's mean words."

Her face changes then from exasperated to something else, something soft. I can't name it, and the emotion is there and gone in a blink of an eye.

"Do you want to have breakfast with us? You'll have to be on your best behavior. No snapping at anyone or telling them that you're a wolf and we're mates," She says, and I shake my head.

"I can't promise that. If she talks to you that way again, I will snap at her. No one hurts my mate."

"Okay then. I guess I'll see you later."

"No, you come with me."

"What?" She asks, pausing with her hand on the doorknob.

"Come with me. I'll show you around town. I'll feed you."

"I would get to avoid my dad and Susan for longer," she says, debating it in her head.

I hold my breath, praying that she picks me. I know that her choosing me over two people she doesn't seem too fond of right now doesn't mean much, but still, it feels like something.

"Okay. I'll tell them that I'm going out," she says. "I'm sure that they won't mind."

She sounds bitter again when she says that last part, and I wonder if maybe I messed up and should have tried to make nice with her family.

It's too late now.

My wolf is happy, spinning in circles inside of me at the thought of being alone with Parker, and I smile.

I can do this. I can make Parker mine.

EIGHT

Parker

"WHAT MADE YOU MOVE TO ALASKA?" I ask Jax as I sit on one of the barstools at his kitchen counter.

"I just wanted to get away from Chicago and my family. Alaska seemed like the exact opposite of a big city. Plus, I had heard good things about the pack here. I always figured I could try it for a few months and move somewhere else if I didn't like it."

"But you like it here?" I ask, and he nods.

"Yeah, this is home now. Unless you hate it!" He hurries to add. "Then I'll move."

"I like it," I tell him, and he relaxes.

I actually do like this little town. I just spent the whole day with Jax, and while it may have started out a little awkward on the ride down the mountain, I slowly started to relax. He showed me around downtown Aspen Ridge, and we grabbed breakfast at this cute little diner before he showed me around the pack's land.

He told me more about shifters and mates. I had wanted to ask to see his wolf again but had chickened out. Even though I've seen him shift with my own eyes, it's like a part of my brain still can't believe it.

After the tour, we came back to his house. He keeps calling it our place, and hearing him say that so easily does something to me. Hell, just being around him does something to me.

I always thought I would find someone who would make me laugh and share my sense of humor. I thought that I would fall for someone who was the life of the party. Instead, it looks like I might just be falling for the person who makes sure everyone gets home safe from the party.

He's so literal, and it was kind of annoying at first, but now I just find it cute. Whatever he says, I know he means. Plus, he can be surprisingly funny.

"Knock, knock," he says, and I grin.

He's been telling me these jokes all day, and it might be dorky, but I love it. I see him glance at his phone screen, reading the rest of the joke, and I smile wider. I figured out he had googled jokes and was reading off of a list after the second knock, knock joke, but I haven't said anything. I like that he's trying to do something nice for me.

He's so awkward with the jokes, and half of the time, he bungles the punchline, but he's trying so hard.

"Who's there?" I ask.

"Interrupting cow."

"Interrupting cow who," I say, already grinning because I know he's about to mess it up.

"Mooo... oh, wait. I think I was supposed to say that when you said interrupting cow who," he says, frowning down at his phone.

"Oh," I say, drawing out the word. "I get it! That's so funny!"

It's a total lie. I've heard that joke a million times since I was a kid, but it makes Jax relax, and he smiles.

"It is, isn't it," he agrees, and I just laugh harder.

Jax goes back to making us dinner, and I turn to take in his house once more. He gave me the tour when we first got here, but I was distracted and didn't really take my time to look around.

It's not what I expected from the man that I was concerned was crazy or a robot. The place is warm and inviting, with cozy rugs and throw blankets. There are no pictures on the walls, and after he told me about his parents, I kind of got why.

He's lonely, just like me. I think that's what made me initially let my guard down, but it's been a fast fall ever since.

Jax is just so sweet. He would do anything to make me smile, and that means a lot to me. When was the last time that someone tried with me? Really tried? It's been forever. I forgot how nice it is.

His eyes stray to my legs when I stand up, and he swallows hard. Seeing the effect that I have on him really does make me feel like the most beautiful woman in the world. He's said that at least five times since this morning, and with each time, I start to believe him a little more.

I always knew I was cute, but I guess I thought that I was too chubby or curvy to be beautiful. Jax sees me differently, though, and I love how I look through his eyes.

"Can I give you a hand with anything?" I ask.

"That's what she said," he blurts out, and I laugh.

He's getting better at being funny, and he seems more relaxed. I thought maybe it was just because we were at his place, but maybe he's starting to feel more at ease around me too.

"Want me to do anything?" I try again, and he shakes his head.

"I've got it. I like taking care of you," he admits, and I nod.

"Okay."

I fill up my water glass, and he frowns like he's upset that he didn't think to do that for me before I had to get up.

"When did your dad and Susan get married?" He asks me, and I love how he says Susan with so much disdain.

It's like I finally have someone on my side, someone who sees just how awful she is.

"A few weeks ago. I was at culinary school, so I missed the actual ceremony, though I've seen the pictures."

"Your dad didn't wait for you to get married?" He asks with a scowl, and I shake my head, taking a drink of water.

"No," I whisper, and he frowns.

"Mate, er, Parker," he corrects, and I blink hard.

"We used to be close," I say because I can see he's about to scoop me up into his arms.

"What happened?" He asks, gripping the knife in his hand tighter.

"My mom died when I was a kid, and we kind of clung to each other after that. It was the two of us against the world, you know?"

"Not really," he admits, and my heart breaks for him.

"Jax..."

"Tell me what happened," he says.

"I don't even know. I graduated high school and things were fine. I worked for a year and we lived together and things were still great between us. Then I left for culinary school, and I'm gone a few months only to come home to Susan. Now I can't help but wonder if things weren't as great as I thought. Maybe I made it all up in my head. Maybe the rose colored glasses are coming off and I'm starting to see the truth."

"Maybe he was lonely," Jax says quietly, and I can hear the own loneliness in his voice.

"Maybe, but why Susan? She's the absolute worst. I mean, if you were lonely, you wouldn't just pick the first woman to look at you, right?"

"I'll only ever choose you," he says.

"But if you were normal," I amend.

I regret the words as soon as they're out. He flinches like I slapped him and my stomach drops.

"No! That's not what I mean. You are normal, Jax. I just meant if you weren't a shifter. If you could choose who you fell for and it wasn't decided by fate."

"I would still only choose you," he says, and my stomach flips upside down.

"How can you be so sure?" I whisper.

"Gut feeling. Plus, I have eyes and you're gorgeous. I'd have to fight off so many men, but I'd still choose you. Every time."

"Maybe that's how my dad feels about Susan," I muse, and Jax snorts.

"That shrew?" He asks. and I grin.

"She really is awful."

"The absolute worst," he agrees, and I smile. "So, culinary school?"

I'm glad that he changed the subject, trying to steer us to safer territory.

"Yeah, I've always loved cooking. It calms me, I guess. I actually specialized in baking though."

"Are you going to open your own place?" He asks, and a ball forms in my stomach.

"That was the plan, but now I don't know. I haven't decided yet," I hedge.

"I think that you would be successful at it. People like you, and I'm sure that you're an amazing baker," he says sincerely and it feels like someone just punched me in the chest.

My dream was to open my own bakery, but when I had told my dad about that, he hadn't seemed too keen on the idea. I still remember what he said, it's burned into my brain.

"That's pretty risky, sweetheart. What happens if it goes under? That's a lot of money to bet on a dream."

It had crushed my heart and my dream of my own bakery all in the blink of an eye. Yet, here is Jax, encouraging me to do what I love.

"I'm not sure. It's scary to bet on yourself like that," I admit, and he frowns.

"You'll do great. I'll look and see if there's any storefronts available in town. Then we should do a benefits analysis and see which location would do best. I'm thinking in the middle of downtown. You could set up an online store too and mail things. I'm not sure about website or social media, but I can learn and help out," he rambles on, and I can see him getting excited for me.

For some reason, seeing that look in his eyes, that bright, hopeful look that's tinged with so much pride in me makes me want to cry. I haven't had someone believe in me that much since my mom passed.

"Maybe you could do a YouTube channel or something. A cooking show!" Jax lists off, and I laugh.

"Maybe. I'll have to think about it. I didn't realize that I had so many options," I joke, and he smiles.

"We'll figure it out."

I know that he means it. He will support me no matter what I want to do.

Jax plates the food, and as he slides my plate in front of me, I can't help but think that just like he would always choose me, I would choose him every time too.

NINE

Jax

I WAKE up with Parker sprawled across me, and my wolf and I are in heaven. This is how we should wake up together every morning. I only wish we were in our bed instead of on the couch.

We watched a movie together last night and she fell asleep on me. I was too afraid to move and wake her up so I fell asleep on the couch too. My neck is paying for it this morning, but it was worth it to be close to her all night.

My wolf is on his feet and pacing inside of me. He's counting down the hours until tonight, and I grit my teeth. Already I can feel the mating heat starting. I wanted Parker from the moment I saw her, but it's nothing compared to how I feel today.

The mating moon is tonight, and I know I need to tell her about it. I need to explain what will happen.

I wonder if she'll be able to feel the pull too?

What if she still doesn't want to be with me? Maybe I

should drive her back to the ski lodge. She can lock herself in her room, and I can do my best to keep my wolf in check and away from her. It will be torture, but I would do it for my mate. I'd do anything for her.

Parker starts to stir against my chest, and I tighten my hold on her so she doesn't roll off the couch.

"Morning," I say, my voice still raspy with sleep.

"Morning. What time is it?"

"A little after eight."

"Ugh, I should call my dad and let him know that I'm okay," she groans.

She sits up, and I watch as she stretches.

"You're a pretty good pillow," she teases, and I smile.

"You can sleep on me anytime."

"Are you working today?" She asks, and I nod.

I told her my schedule yesterday. I hate to be away from her for even a second, but I know without asking that she's not going to let me take her to the hospital with me.

"You can stay here today. I'll leave you my car, and you can hang out and avoid your dad and Susan some more," I offer.

"Okay, but I should go back and change at least," she says, yawning.

"You can borrow some of my clothes too. Or I can go get your suitcase before work if you want."

"No, I'm sure I'll have to have lunch with them or something. I'll grab my things then. Are you sure you won't need your car, though?"

"I'll ask Roman to pick me up. He lives close by, and we work the same shift today," I say, already sending him a text.

He sends back a thumbs up and says he'll be here in twenty.

"Okay," she says, nodding.

She moves to stand, and I reach out, grabbing her hand and tugging her back down. She gasps when our skin touches, and I know then that she must be able to feel the mating heat too. At least to some extent.

"I... I need to tell you something," I start, and she nods.

"Okay, what's up?"

My hand flexes around hers, and I rub my thumb back and forth on the back of her hand, trying to calm my nerves.

"Tonight is the full moon," I say, and she blinks.

"Okay..."

"It's also the mating moon."

"The what?"

"The mating moon. All mated shifters, on every full moon, experience this... well, this pull. It's called the mating heat... and um..."

"Jax, spit it out," Parker says, and I swallow hard.

"And basically, they all fuck like rabbits," I blurt, and she stares at me for a beat.

"We're going to fuck like rabbits?" She asks, and I want to kiss her so badly.

"I hope," I admit, and she smiles. "I'm doing a terrible job explaining all of this, but yes. All shifters and their mates feel this heat; this need to mate. We don't have to do anything! I just wanted to explain what you might be feeling. It will get stronger as the day goes on and the full moon rises."

"Okay, and if I say no?"

"Then we can just hang out and watch a movie again."

I'll go crazy trying to keep my hands to myself, but I'll do it.

"And if I say yes?" She asks, her voice coming out husky with need.

"Then my wolf and I claim you."

She studies me, nodding, and I swallow. I want to ask her which it will be, but I don't want to push her. She may still need time to decide.

"I have to shower and get to the hospital. Do you want me to make you breakfast before I go?" I offer.

"You know, I did go to culinary school. Maybe I should be making you breakfast," she retorts.

"If you'd like. You can do anything you want here."

She nods and then shocks the hell out of me by standing, moving between my legs, and dropping a quick kiss on my surprised lips.

She smiles and heads into the kitchen, and I hurry to follow her.

"What was that for?" I ask her, and she smiles.

"Just because I felt like it," she says easily, and I growl.

"But what made you feel like doing it?"

"Why does it matter?"

"Because I want to do it over and over again," I say, exasperated.

She giggles, and the sound sends vibrations down my spine.

"Can I kiss you whenever I want too?" I ask her, and she looks at me slyly over her shoulder.

"Depends," she says, and I tense.

"On what?"

"On if you can catch me," she says.

She takes off down the hallway, and I'm on her like she's my prey. She is, in a way, and I grin as I catch up to her, wrapping my arms around her waist and sweeping her off her feet.

She wraps her legs around my waist, laughing as I back

her up against the front door. We're eye level now, and she licks her plump lips.

"Jax," she whispers, and my name sounds like a promise on her lips.

I cup the back of her neck and pull her in for a devastating kiss. My lips land on hers a second later, and I forget about everything. This, this is what I was missing. Someone to make me laugh, to make me smile. She makes me feel whole. She makes this place feel like a home.

Parker moans, her fingers tangling in my hair as I grin against her. Her lips open underneath mine and I slip my tongue into her mouth. The scent and taste of sugar are all around me and I want to drown in it, in her.

Our lips part, both of us hungry and needing more, more, *more*. That's the only thought in my head as I plunder her mouth.

Electricity shoots through my veins, sparking my nerve endings along the way and making me crave my mate even more. I didn't even think that was possible, but with every gasp and moan that falls from Parker's lips, I become even more obsessed with her. She's in my bloodstream now, a part of me just like my wolf.

"Mine," I growl against her mouth, and she hums in her throat.

Her fingers tighten in my hair and she tugs my mouth back to hers. I'm so lost in her that I don't notice Roman pulling up out front or him walking to the front door. It isn't until he's ringing the doorbell and yelling for me to hurry up that I come back to Earth.

"Shit," I groan. "I have to go to work."

"I'll be here when you get back," she promises, and I kiss her once more before I set her on her feet.

We're both breathing hard, and my wolf is begging me

to blow off work and make her come so many times that we both lose track.

Her phone starts to ring, and she heads to grab it while I open the door.

"Hey, I just need to change and take a quick shower," I tell him, and he nods.

"How's everything going with your mate?" He asks me as he steps inside.

"Good. She's here," I say, pride swelling in my chest.

"Congrats, man," he says with a smile, and I grin.

"Thanks."

"Now, hurry up and get ready. We're going to be late, and Micah and Asher will end up giving us shit all week."

"I'll be right back," I promise as I race upstairs to get ready.

My thoughts are on Parker as I take the fastest shower of my life. Then I pull on a pair of track pants and a t-shirt and jog back downstairs.

Parker and Roman are in the kitchen talking. Jealousy starts to rise inside of me before I remember that Roman is already mated. He's left the whole island between them, and I appreciate the space.

"I've got to go, but call me if you need anything. I'll be back tonight at nine."

"Okay, have a good day," she tells me, and I can't help but lean down and steal one more kiss from her.

"See you tonight," I whisper against her lips, and she smiles.

Roman is waiting for me by the front door, and I hurry to follow him outside.

"Thanks for the ride," I tell him as we head to the hospital.

"No problem. Are you ready for tonight?" He asks me, and I wipe my hands on my pants.

"I think so," I say as I turn to look out the window.

I hope so...

TEN

Parker

I TRIED to call my dad, but he didn't answer. I feel bad saying it, but I was actually glad when he didn't answer or call me back right away. I didn't really want to see them today and have them ruin my buzz.

I've felt like I was floating on a cloud all day. I floated around Jax's place for a few hours, enjoying the quiet early morning.

It's so beautiful here in Aspen Ridge. I can see why Jax fell in love with this place. The mountains form a natural border around the land, and it's dotted with pine trees and pretty meadows that are starting to bloom now that the snow is starting to melt. There's still snow on the mountains, though, and it creates a breathtaking view.

I made lunch here and then made the drive back up to the ski lodge to grab a change of clothes. When I got there, I was just going to shower and change my clothes, but I knew then that I wasn't going back there tonight.

I want Jax.

Maybe it's the mating moon, but I doubt it. I was attracted to Jax when I saw him in the hospital, and my feelings have been growing ever since. Sure, I was fighting those feelings and kind of wary of him in the beginning, but then I got to know him.

He's not the cold robot or the crazy man I first thought he was. He's sweet and attentive. He makes me laugh and feel beautiful. He makes me feel like the most important person in the world to him. I haven't felt lonely or depressed since I met him.

It's more than that, though. He makes me feel things that I've never felt before. It's like I'm burning up from the inside. There's an ache, an unfamiliar tug in my stomach every time he's close to me.

I've never kissed anyone in my life, and yet I couldn't seem to stop myself from kissing him this morning. I wasn't self-conscious or worried about doing it wrong. I just trusted my gut, and it paid off.

Being in his arms, had felt so right. When he had pinned me against the door and pressed his body against mine, that needy ache between my legs had grown so much that I was seconds away from begging him to fuck me right then and there.

Too bad for me, his friend had come to pick him up. He was gone after one more kiss, leaving me a horny mess.

Now it's almost nine. I made a late dinner so Jax can eat whenever he gets home. My eyes stray to the clock, and anticipation floods my system as I see that Jax should be home in five minutes.

The mating heat or something else is starting to hit me, and all I can think about is jumping Jax's bones as soon as he walks in the door.

Maybe I should go upstairs and strip. I could be waiting for him in bed, I think, with a devilish smile.

I'm about to do just that when headlights flash across the front windows. My toes curl, and I hold my breath as Jax comes to the front door.

He kicks the door open, and my breath comes out in a rush.

My mate... he looks wild, almost feral. At this moment, he is the predator and I'm his prey. His blue eyes are dark and filled with wicked promise.

Already I can feel myself responding to the heat in his gaze. My body warms, and I'm breathing hard already without even taking a step. My nipples tighten into painful peaks, and I can feel my panties growing damp with my arousal.

"Jax," I beg, and he kicks the door shut, stalking toward me.

"Mate," he growls, and I almost sob as I get ready to throw myself at him.

ELEVEN

Jax

I'VE BEEN on edge all day as the mating heat started to bear down on me. I knew I would feel it, but I never thought it would be this strong. I'm having a hard time controlling myself, but I manage to hold my wolf and me back from taking her on the foyer floor.

I need to talk to her and make sure she wants this too. That she chooses me too. I would never force Parker to do anything she doesn't want.

I wonder if she can feel it too, the mating heat. My eyes rake down her body, taking in her pebbled nipples and the way she keeps licking her lips and pressing her thighs together.

Yes, she can feel it too.

Knowing that she can feel the attraction, too, makes me feel better, but it also makes holding myself and my wolf back harder.

I couldn't stop picturing fucking her all day. We're lucky the hospital was quiet.

I want to feel her under me, her warm body welcoming my thrusts as I claim her. I want her to ride me, her black hair surrounding us as she bounces up and down on my cock. Once she's creamed all over my cock, I'll flip her onto her hands and knees and plow into her from behind, gripping her hips as I slam into her.

I have so many plans for her, but I need to make sure she's on the same page as me first.

"Parker," I say as I continue to stalk toward her.

Her name comes out more like a growl, but that doesn't scare her.

"Yes! Yes, please," she says, throwing herself at me.

I catch her easily, and my wolf roars in my head as I pin her against the nearest available surface. Her eyes are heavy and dark with lust, and my wolf whines, wanting to claim her. *Mate, mate, mate,* he chants in my head as I drink in the sight of her. I can smell her desire as it fills the room, and my mouth starts to water at the scent.

I can feel my canines start to elongate as the mating heat threatens to consume me. Parker lets out a whine, wiggling against my cock, and my heart is beating out of control in my chest. My whole being is yearning to claim her. The desire is too much for me. Her too, apparently because a second later, she throws her head back and lets out a moan, her fingers tangling in my hair as she rides the ridge behind the seam of my jeans.

"Jax, I need you. Please, please, you have to take the ache away," she pleads, and I'm moving in a flash.

I carry her upstairs, taking the stairs two at a time as I race for our bedroom. I want our first time to be in our bed. I want her virginity to stain the sheets so that I can frame them and remember the best night of my life.

My lips slam down on hers as I lay her down on the bed, and she clings to me, moaning into the kiss. It feels more like a branding, and my wolf howls at the thought.

I devour her as the mating heat beats down against my back. My tongue presses against the seam of her lips, and she opens for me, just as greedy for me as I am for her. I eat at her mouth until I feel her tiny fingers start to tug at my clothes.

I stand by the bed, tearing at my clothes in my haste to get inside her. I get my jeans off, but I don't have time to wrestle with my shirt or boxers, and I claw at the thin fabric, ripping them to shreds and throwing them at my feet.

Parker is stripping just as fast, and she collapses back against the mattress, spreading out in the center of the bed, her black hair like a dark cloud around her head. Her eyes remind me of the ocean on a stormy day, and my wolf starts to pace inside me as we take her in.

She's panting in need; her face twisted in a wince as the ache spreads through her. I wanted to go slow, be gentle with her, and make this first time good for her, but I can't stand to see her in pain, and that wins out.

I spread her thighs wide as I climb up on the bed. My fingers trail up her thighs, and I dip my thumb into her center, testing to make sure she's ready for me and growling as I feel how drenched she is. My wolf howls at the scent, breathing deep, and the sight of her glistening lips spread wide and inviting before me.

My animal is taking over, and I bracket her body with my arms as I lean down and sink my teeth into the space where her neck and shoulder meet. She lets out a scream, moaning as pleasure courses through her, and I take the opportunity to sink into her. She screams again as I take her cherry, and I feel her come as soon as I'm fully seated inside her.

Her walls are gripping me so tightly as I lick over the bite mark and seal it. It's in the same spot as before, and I wish I had done it on her other side. I wish she was covered in my marks so everyone knows she's mine.

I don't give her time to adjust before I draw my hips back and slam back into her. I fuck her hard as I lick and nuzzle against the mark. It's sensitive, and she comes every time I brush over it. I've lost track of how many orgasms she's had, but I promise myself that I'll keep track in the future. My wolf howls, pleased that we can give our mate so much pleasure.

The base of my spine starts to tingle, and I know I'm about to come too. I want us to go off together, and I grip one of her thighs, hoisting it higher on my hip as I rut into her, making sure to hit her clit with every stroke. I can feel her start to spasm around my length, and I groan when I feel her start to come again. I lean down and brush against my mark as I find my own release, coming deep inside her.

I roll us so I don't crush her, and Parker braces her hands against my chest, rocking her hips as soon as she gets on top.

"I need more," she moans, and I grip her hips, helping her find her rhythm.

"Whatever you need, mate. It's yours. I'm all yours."

She bounces on my cock, throwing her head back until I can feel her silky hair tickling the top of my thighs. My hands cup her tits, rolling the pebbled nipples between my fingers as she rides me. I lean up, taking one of the tips into my mouth and rolling it against my tongue. I bite down gently and am rewarded when she comes on my cock again.

"Jax, I need you," she pants, and I release her nipple.

"What do you need, mate?"

"Touch the mark," she begs, and I lean forward at once, running my lips over the bite mark.

She goes off again, and her pussy sucks another orgasm from me.

"Don't stop," she pleads, and I roll us again.

I pull out, and she whines, looking at me over her shoulder as I flip her onto her stomach and pull her up onto her hands and knees. I sink back inside her pussy, gripping her hips as I pound into her. She moans, throwing her head back, and I look up into the mirror above the dresser, and our eyes meet. She watches me as I mount her and claim her, and I swear it feels like our souls are joining as she orgasms again and then again.

I love how she's just as insatiable for me as I am for her, and I grin to myself as my wolf and I realize that the night is just getting started.

TWELVE

Jax

"HOW WAS your first night as a mated man?" Micah asks as he hops up on the front counter next to me.

"Very good," I say, and he grins.

"I bet. Lucky bastard," he teases me, and I roll my eyes.

"Iggy can't wait to meet Parker," Roman tells me, and I look up, smiling.

"I'm sure Parker will love her. We'll have to get them together soon."

"Is she all moved in then? Or do you have to go back home with her and get her things?" Roman asks.

"I...I'm not sure what we'll do with her things," I say.

The truth is that I've been so wrapped up in my new mate that I haven't been thinking about the next steps. Roman is right, though. I need to figure out how to get Parker moved in here. Then I need to look for properties in town for her bakery in case she wants to open her own place. Maybe I should start looking into a YouTube channel too.

I make a mental to-do list in my head as my friends lean against the front reception desk. I'm almost done with my shift. If Micah is already here, then it must be time for me to get ready to leave.

"Is Asher here yet?" Roman asks.

"Yeah, he was getting changed," Micah says, pulling out a granola bar and biting off half of it in one go.

Asher walks up then, looking exhausted, and I wonder what kept him up last night.

"I bet I'm next," Micah teases Asher, and he shrugs.

"Go for it," he drawls.

Out of the four of us, Asher is the only one who doesn't seem at all interested in finding his fated mate. He's never been out looking for her, never showed any interest when the rest of us talked about it.

Micah pretends like he wants it, but even now, I can see the fear and worry in his eyes. Something is scaring him, but I don't know what.

"I just finished up my paperwork so I'm going to head out," Roman says, interrupting my thoughts, and I nod.

"Me too. Have a good shift, guys."

I wave at Asher and Micah and trail after Roman to the locker room. We both get changed, and I see Roman smiling out of the corner of my eye.

"Headed home to see Iggy?" I guess, and he nods.

"Yeah. How are you and Parker doing?" He asks.

We talked a bit about last night during our shift. He knows that I claimed her, that she seemed happy this morning, but that's it.

"I haven't talked to her about staying here yet. Well, I have, but I haven't made sure that she wants to."

"Okay, so go home and ask her tonight. I'm sure that you two can figure something out. Let me know if you need help moving her in," he offers, and I nod.

"I will, thanks."

We head out the backdoor to the employee parking lot, and he waves at me as he heads over to his car. I climb into my SUV and make the short drive home. The entire way, I'm practicing what I want to say in my head, laying out my case for why she should move here to Aspen Ridge, but the truth is that I'll follow her anywhere.

The house smells like garlic and tomatoes when I walk in, and my wolf and I both lick our lips. I can still smell Parker's candy sweet scent over it all, and I instantly want to be inside her again.

"It smells good in here," I say as I head into the kitchen to greet my mate.

"Thanks. I was craving lasagna," she says with a bright smile.

She looks so at home in my kitchen, and hope swells inside me. She seems to like it here. Maybe this won't be a hard conversation.

"Do you need help with anything?"

"Nope, you're just in time. I'm about to take out the garlic bread, and then it will be time to eat."

"I'm going to go take a quick shower. I'll be right back down."

She nods distractedly, grating some parmesan cheese into a bowl as I head upstairs. Her scent is here, too, and I inhale deeply. I love this house, but I'd be okay with moving if it meant being with Parker.

I take a quick shower and then jog back downstairs to see Parker setting the food out on the table.

"Dig in," she says, smiling at me, and I grab her, pulling her into my arms and kissing her.

I meant it to be a quick peek, but just like every other time I'm close to her, I lose control.

My hands find their way around her waist, and I pull her tighter against me until her curves are pressed firmly against the hard lines of my body. My wolf whines, wanting to rut into her, and I force myself to slow down.

My wolf growls when I loosen my hold on her. He's urging me to pin her beneath us and claim her again, but I hold him back. We need to talk first. Then I can focus entirely on my mate.

He snorts, pacing inside of me, and I break the kiss.

"I meant dig into the food," she jokes, and I smile.

"Couldn't resist."

We take our seats, and I put a slice of lasagna on Parker's plate before doing my own.

"How was work?" She asks.

"Slow. I was on shift with Roman, though, so it was nice to hang out with him."

"Yeah, it's cool that you have such a close friend at work."

"We talked about you," I start, shifting awkwardly in my chair.

"Yeah? All good things, I'm sure," she jokes, and I crack a smile.

"There's only good things about you," I tell her honestly.

She smiles softly at me, and I clear my throat.

"They asked if you were moving here..." I say, trailing off.

I'm trying to read her facial expression and gauge her

reaction, but her face is blank. She seems surprised by the question initially.

"I... I haven't figured that out yet," she finally admits, and I shift again in my chair.

"Are you leaving tomorrow with your dad and Susan?" I ask her, and she chews on her plump bottom lip.

"I don't know. I don't know what to do," she says, staring down at her plate.

She's moving her food around as she thinks about it, and I wish I knew how to help her. I hate seeing her upset like this.

"It still... it still seems crazy to move in with you after only knowing you a few days. I know we're fated and all of that, but there's just... I don't know. It feels like I'm giving up all of my old life, everything I know, to be here."

"And I'm not worth it."

I don't even realize I've said it out loud until her eyes start to well with tears.

"You are, Jax. It's just a really big decision."

Her phone starts to ring, and she blinks, trying to wipe away the tears as she stands to answer it.

"It's my dad," she whispers, and I tense even more.

"Hello?" She answers. "What? No, I..."

I can hear the confusion and then the sadness in her voice, and it kills me. I'm on my feet and at her side in the blink of an eye. I can hear part of the conversation, especially when Susan starts yelling. Her shrill voice hurts my ears, and my wolf whines, wanting her to stop.

"Get back here now! We paid for this vacation so that you could get to know Susan, and instead, you've been holed up with some man you just met!"

"Like a whore!" Susan adds, and my wolf and I growl.

"She's not a whore!" I yell back, and Parker jumps, turning to stare up at me.

Pain and a fresh wave of tears are in her eyes, and I take the phone from her, ending the call.

"You aren't. You're perfect. Don't listen to them, mate," I tell her, trying to soothe her.

"They're still trying to treat me like I'm a little kid or something. They want me to get to know Susan, but they don't know anything about me either," she says, and I nod, pulling her into my arms.

"I know, Parker, I know," I say, swallowing hard.

I rack my brain, trying to think of something to say or do to make her feel better.

"Knock, knock," I blurt out, and she smiles.

I've been spending my breaks at the hospital memorizing a few jokes since Parker seems to love them so much.

"Who's there?

"Cow says."

"Cow says who?" She asks, and she's starting to look more like her usual happy self.

"No, a cow says moo," I say, and she grins up at me.

"Thanks, Jax," she whispers, wrapping her arms around my waist.

I rub my hands up and down her back, not noticing how close we are to the table and the pan of lasagna until it's too late.

My hand hits the dish, sending cheese and pasta sauce onto the ground and our legs.

"Shit!" I say, grabbing the pan before it can tip all the way over.

"Your hand!" Parker yells, jerking my hand away from the hot pan.

"I'm fine," I promise her.

She still looks at it, and my wolf perks up inside of me. He loves having her hands on us.

"I'm really fine, but we should both probably get cleaned up," I say, looking down at our legs and feet that are now splattered with red sauce.

THIRTEEN

Parker

"COME ON, COME SHOWER WITH ME," Jax says softly, and I nod, letting him lead me upstairs and into our bedroom.

Our?

We walk into the bathroom and start to strip. As soon as he's naked, he pulls me back into his arms. He must be able to see the panic on my face because he doesn't say anything for a moment, giving me time to think.

My mind is racing a million miles an hour, and I don't know what to do. I can't believe that I'm even thinking about moving here. Is that crazy? I mean, I've only known Jax for three days. Still, I can't deny how I feel about him.

You love him.

That thought has me tensing in his arms, but it's the truth. I know it deep in my gut. I thought that he was crazy when he said that I wouldn't want to leave him after three days, but he was right.

Can I move here, though? Do I want to live in a small town?

As long as I'm with Jax, I think I could be happy. I like Aspen Ridge, or what I've seen of it, anyway. I think that I could love it here.

"We'll do whatever you want, Parker. If you don't want to move here, then that's fine. I'll go wherever you want to go. I can live anywhere, as long as you're there too," he says, and that only has me tearing up even more.

He's attached to this place. He loves it here. He has friends and a career here, yet he'd give it all up for me.

"I love you," I whisper, and he tenses against me.

He tugs on my ponytail until I look up at him, meeting his blue eyes.

"I love you, mate. So much. More than anything," he says, and I smile up at him.

"I know," I admit, and he smiles down at me. "I'll move here. I just want to be with you too."

"Really? Are you sure?" He asks, and I nod.

"I'm sure."

I bite my lip and pull him closer to me, capturing his lips with mine in a sweet kiss.

His lips land on mine then, and I forget all about my dad and Susan and the future. There's only this moment with Jax.

Jax gives me one last kiss before stepping away and turning the shower on. It gives me an opportunity to appreciate my gorgeous, sexy-as-hell man. I love his broad shoulders and defined pecs, the corded muscles in his arms, all of the strength he uses to protect and comfort me. And then there's his cock. His monster cock that looks like it might split me in two. Without even thinking, I lick my lips.

"That's what she said?" Jax asks when he sees where I'm looking, and I burst out laughing.

"Yeah," I say breathlessly.

He grins at me, so damn happy to have made me laugh. I never stood a chance with him. How could anyone ever resist a man like him?

"Damn, you're so perfect, mate. Need to have you again."

He stalks toward me, and I let him catch me easily because I want him just as badly. Jax kisses me as he glides his hands down my body, squeezing my breasts before continuing his journey south. He surprises me by scooping me up and walking us toward the shower, never breaking the kiss.

Only when we're under the hot spray of water do we both come up for air.

"Parker," he groans. "I love the taste of your lips," he whispers, kissing me again. "Love your smooth skin. So damn soft," he murmurs, kissing down my neck and over my collarbone. "God, and these perfect breasts..." Jax sucks one of my breasts into his mouth while flicking the nipple on my other breast with his thumb. Everything he does drives me crazy with want and need.

"More..." I moan.

Jax kisses lower, kneeling before me. His hands rest on my hips, guiding me backward so I'm leaning against the wall of the shower. He scrapes his teeth along my hip bone and blazes a trail of kisses to my other hip bone, where he sucks and nips the skin. I feel his hands massaging my ass, then gripping lower on my thighs.

So close to where I need him...

Jax guides one leg up over his shoulder, giving him complete access to my soaked pussy. I feel exposed, but not in a bad way. It's hot the way that he's looking at me. He looks like he's about to go out of his mind with need, and I feel the same.

He turns his head and sinks his teeth into the thigh slung over his shoulder, kissing away the sting. Pleasure courses through me, and I bite back a smile. I love when he marks me like that.

"So wet for me, mate," he growls against my skin.

I nod and dig my fingers into his hair, urging him forward. I can feel my arousal dripping down my thighs, and I know he can see and smell it, too.

He chuckles. "You want it bad, don't you, Parker? Want my tongue inside your juicy little pussy?"

Before I can reply, he buries his face in my center and devours me.

He flattens his tongue and runs it from my entrance to my clit. Again. Again. I buck my hips and moan his name.

Jax spears his tongue deep inside my hole, causing my channel to pulse around him and release a wave of wetness. Jax growls, and I feel the vibrations echoing off every nerve in my body. He pulls his tongue out and thrusts it back in, fucking me with his mouth while rubbing my clit with his thumb. It's almost too much; I feel myself getting close already. So close...

Jax withdraws his tongue and finger, and I cry out at the loss.

"I've got you, love. I'll always take care of you. Always. "

Jax licks my tight ball of nerves, drawing figure eights with his tongue, over and over. And then he slams two fingers in my hole, and my body jerks, back arching off of the tile wall of the shower. Jax moves his other hand from my hip to my stomach, spreading his fingers out over my abdomen and keeping me pinned to the wall while also intensifying the pressure I feel building again deep in my core.

"J-Jax, don't stop, please. Oh, god!"

He pumps his fingers faster, curling them up and hitting that super-sensitive spot inside me. My thighs jerk together, and he strokes the spot again.

"Ah, ah, too much..."

"I've got you; let go for me," he purrs. "Come all over my face."

He returns his attention to my clit, alternating between fast and slow, hard and soft licks. Then, he sucks my little nub into his mouth and softly bites down. That's it. That's all it takes to have my orgasm ripping through me.

"Oh fuck, Jax, I..."

My knees buckle, and Jax catches me, easily holding me up. He replaces his fingers with his tongue, lapping up all of my come as my pussy convulses around him, squeezing his tongue as he massages my walls. I can feel the stress and heartbreak from the last few days melt off my bones and pool in my core, dripping out of me as Jax sucks it all in.

The last of my orgasm fades, and I slump against Jax. He stands up and kisses me long, deep, slow, and passionate. He slides his hands up to my hips, and I throw my arms around his neck, forcing the kiss to go deeper.

He finally breaks the kiss and nuzzles my neck, kissing my shoulder and licking over the bite mark there.

"You're so fucking sexy. Love watching you come apart in my hands, in my mouth. The most beautiful thing that I've ever seen."

Jax rests his forehead on mine. We're both breathing heavily, sharing the same air and the same passion. I slide my hands down his neck, over his chest and well-defined abs, and grip his hard cock. He hisses and throws his head back.

"Your turn," I grin up at him.

"Shit, Parker..."

I have no idea what I'm doing, but my body takes over. My only goal now is pleasing my mate. I kneel before him, and he puts his hands on the wall in front of him to steady himself. I stroke his intimidatingly thick cock a few more times and then lick the drop of precum at the very tip.

"Fuck!" Jax clenches his jaw, and I see the muscles in his neck strain.

I feel so powerful, even on my knees. I open my mouth and slowly ease as much of him into me as I can. He squeezes his eyes shut and throws his head back. I love knowing I am giving him this pleasure.

"That's it, that's so fucking it..."

When his length hits the back of my throat, I swallow him down. Jax's eyes flash open, and a guttural moan rips out of him.

I continue to suck and swallow, massaging his massive length. He looks down at me with such awe, and I can't wait to taste him exploding in my mouth.

Jax, however, has other plans.

He pulls out of my mouth with a pop and lifts me into his arms.

"You're incredible, but I *need* to come inside of your perfect pussy."

Before I can respond, he captures my mouth in a frantic kiss while guiding me backward until my back hits the wall. He breaks the kiss to lift me into his arms. My legs automatically wrap around his hips, and I feel his hard cock rub up and down my slit.

"Yes, mate, Jax," I encourage, grinding down on him.

He growls but continues to slide his length through my folds, not penetrating me. His cock scrapes across my clit, winding that coil deep within tighter and tighter with each stroke. I feel his mouth roam over my neck, chest, nipples, and everywhere in between. The heat of his tongue and the sting of his teeth peppering my skin sets my nerves on fire. My fingers tangle in his hair as I hold on for dear life.

Finally, *finally,* he thrusts his cock deep inside of me while biting down on my nipple. I gasp and throw my head back while clinging to my mate. I'm still so sore from last night, but I want this. I want him.

"I've got you," he murmurs into the side of my neck. "I think you want to come for me, mate." I whimper and grind down on his thick cock, the burning pain of being stretched remarkably adding to my pleasure. "Come for me," Jax demands as he licks my bite mark.

I have no choice but to give in to him. The coil snaps, and I instantly come, pulsing and shaking in his arms. My scream is caught in my throat and I forget to breathe. All I can do is drown in wave after wave of pleasure as it washes over me and leaks out from between my thighs.

"Jesus Christ, Parker, love when you come on my dick, so beautiful, you feel so good."

Jax licks my neck and nibbles at my pulse point. A shiver runs down my spine when I think about him marking me again.

I drag precious air into my lungs, the oxygen pulling pleasure along with it while traveling into my bloodstream and coursing throughout my body.

I hear Jax chuckle as he pulls my earlobe through his teeth.

"Love seeing you lost in pleasure."

All I can do is moan at this point.

Jax pulls out and slams back into me, setting a punishing pace. His fingers tighten around my thighs as he holds me in place, pounding into me again and again. It hurts so good; feeling his cock stretch me, his fingers bruise me, and his teeth sink into my neck.

I gasp and cry out as exquisite pain and pleasure wrap around my body. Jax growls into my skin, then licks his mark over and over. Each swipe of his tongue makes my pussy throb. I'm shaking, sweating, and almost afraid of the orgasm he's pulling from me.

I tilt my head back, and he covers my mouth with his, swallowing my cries in an all-consuming kiss. He rests his forehead on mine, grunting with each thrust of his hips.

"Come for me. One more time. I need you to come."

I close my eyes as I reach the point of no return, then snap my eyes open right as pleasure overtakes my body. Jax's cock swells inside of me and explodes. Another wave of pleasure vibrates through me, through him, through us as we breathe together as one.

"Parker... my mate," he whispers as the last of our orgasm slips away, dripping down between us. The moment lasts forever, we never break eye contact, and I can see every emotion Jax is feeling. I know he can see all of me at this moment, so raw and unfiltered.

Jax sets me down, keeping one hand around my waist while his other hand goes behind me, bracing himself on the wall. We're both still shaking, and it seems Jax is about as unsteady as I am on my feet right now.

He tucks me into his chest, resting his forehead on the wall, covering me with his entire body like he's shielding me from everything outside of this moment. I place a gentle kiss on his chest before burying my head there and wrapping my arms around his waist.

Neither one of us says a word as we separate. Jax grabs the body wash and pours some in his hand before rubbing it all over my body, taking in every curve with such reverence. I do the same to him, soaping up his chest and arms, taking time to memorize the contours of his body.

I love how we take care of each other. I know it makes him happy to care for me, and as I wash the soap from his body, I find that I love it too.

He turns the water off and dries me with a fluffy towel, then pauses to cup my face in his hands, smiling down at me.

I look into his endless blue eyes and see such tenderness and depth. I try to look away, but he turns my face back toward his.

"I love you, my perfect mate."

His eyes are filled with emotion, and I wonder if I look as love drunk as he does.

"I love you, too."

Jax growls in approval and scoops me up in his arms. Moments later, he's tucking me into our bed and crawling in behind me.

He curls around me, and for the first time in my life, I feel like I'm right where I belong.

FOURTEEN

Jax

FIVE YEARS LATER...

I FINISH my shift and practically sprint for the door. I can't wait to get home to my mate and kids. We're leaving tomorrow for a little family vacation, and I can't wait to be away from the hospital for a few days. I'm going to spend as much time as I can with my mate.

My wolf howls inside me as I start the car and head out of the parking lot. He's been so content since we met Parker and got her all moved into our house. I guess waking up beside our mate every morning just puts him in a good mood. Either way, he's been a lot easier to deal with.

I see Roman's car ahead of me, turning towards downtown, and I know he must be headed to pick up Iggy from the bakery. Parker opened The Goody Basket four years ago, and it's been a huge hit in town. I think she was worried, even though I told her not to be. Shifters have a huge sweet tooth, and she's been selling out of things pretty much every day.

I pull up in front of our house and smile when I see our kids' faces in the front window. They jump around as soon as they see my car, and I laugh. They look so much like Parker with their pitch-black hair and blue eyes.

Maddie and Gage both come running into my arms as soon as I step inside, and I laugh, scooping them up. Gage is about to be three, and Maddie just turned two. We had them both close together, and now I think we're done. The two of them are quite a handful.

"Where's mommy?" I ask them, and they point me down the hallway to the kitchen.

I should have known. Parker loves being in the kitchen. I walk in and see my mate and wife standing at the stove, stirring something.

Parker and I got married right after we got back to Aspen Ridge with her things. I think she was a little bummed that her dad wasn't there to help us celebrate, but when I asked her about it, she just reminded me that she wasn't at his wedding either.

The two of them haven't ever made up. Her dad is still married to Susan, and Parker doesn't want her in our life. I'm okay to just follow her lead, but because we won't see Susan, we also don't see her dad either.

I think she used to be sad about it, but she's stopped mentioning them in the last few years. I think that she's at peace now, that she knows that their relationship is never going to go back to where it was the two of them against the world. Too much time and too many things have happened since then.

"Smells good," I say, burying my face in her neck, and she laughs.

"Me or the soup?"

"Both," I answer, and she turns, offering me her lips.

I kiss her, smiling against her mouth when the kids wrap themselves around my legs.

"How was work?" She asks.

"Good. What about you?"

"Busy! We tried a new brownie recipe today, and it was a big hit."

"Another success," I say, and she smiles.

I've always been sure to support her in everything because it makes her smile like that. It's not like it's hard to believe in her. Everything that she's done has been a success.

"Are you all packed for tomorrow?" I ask her, and she nods.

"Yeah, I did the kids' things this afternoon, and the last of my stuff is in the dryer. I just need to fold it and put it in the suitcase."

"I can do that for you," I tell her, and she smiles.

"Thanks, Jax."

I steal one more kiss before I start to walk around the kitchen with both of our kids wrapped around my legs. They're sitting on my feet, wigging and giggling with every step.

"Getting your workout in today, I see," Parker jokes, and I laugh.

Gage slips off, and Maddie tips over right after him. They're laughing together on the floor, and my wolf and I sigh happily. I never really thought that I could be this happy. I just thought I would be settled once I found my mate, but having Parker and the kids is the best thing that has ever happened to me.

"Why don't you color daddy a picture? He was just telling me that his locker at work was looking a little empty," Parker says, and the kids race off to grab the arts and crafts supplies.

I smile. My locker is covered in the kids' artwork. I think I have everything that they've ever made me there. It's practically wallpaper now.

"Laundry, please?" Parker says as she bends to grab the tray of brownies out of the oven.

"On it," I say, heading that way.

I head into the laundry room, reaching into the dryer and coming out with a handful of lace. I blink, and it takes me a second to realize what the scraps of lace and silk are. Then I'm grinning.

My wolf howls inside me as I pull out the rest of the lingerie, and turn, looking over my shoulder at Parker.

"Which do you think I should pack, and what should I wear tonight?" She purrs, and I turn, prowling toward her.

"I'll pack all of it. You won't be wearing it long enough tonight for me to enjoy it," I growl against her lips, and she smirks.

"What about right now?" She whispers, and I groan as I kick the laundry room door closed behind us and get lost in my wife.

Looking for the rest of the Aspen Ridge Pack: Shifter M.D. series? Check them out here!

Bitten By The Doctor
Fated To The Doctor
Marked By The Doctor

Be sure to check out the Aspen Ridge Pack:
Loners
The Grizzlies Captive Mate

WANT A FREE BOOK?

Want a free copy of Wolf Lover? It's a steamy, scarred military hero, curvy girl romance! Check it out today here!

ABOUT THE AUTHOR

CONNECT WITH ME!

If you enjoyed this story, please consider leaving a review on Amazon or any other reader site or blog that you like. Don't forget to recommend it to your other reader friends.

If you want to chat with me, please consider joining my VIP list or connecting with me on one of my Social Media platforms. I love talking with each of my readers. Links below!

Website

ALSO BY LUNA WILDER

Aspen Ridge Pack: Shifter M.D.

Bitten By The Doctor

Bound To The Doctor

Fated To The Doctor

Marked By The Doctor

Aspen Ridge Pack: Loners

The Grizzlies Captive Mate

www.ingramcontent.com/pod-product-compliance
Ingram Content Group UK Ltd.
Pitfield, Milton Keynes, MK11 3LW, UK
UKHW040011200726
13854UKWH00001B/147

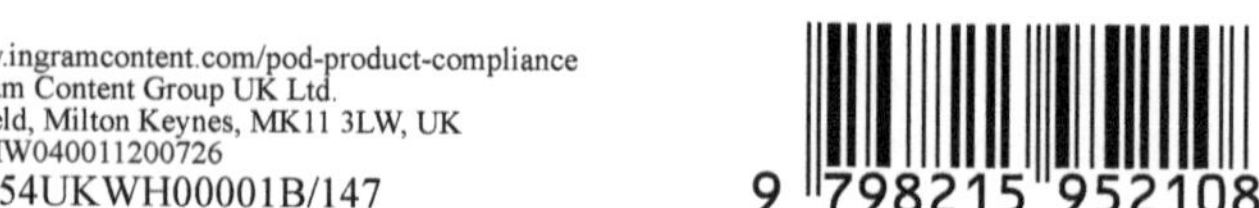